Jelly Roll

Mere Joyce

orca currents

ORCA BOOK PUBLISHERS

Published in Canada and the United States in 2020 by Orca Book Publishers.
orcabook.com

Library and Archives Canada Cataloguing in Publication
Title: Jelly roll / Mere Joyce.
Names: Joyce, Mere, 1988– author.
Series: Orca currents.
Description: Series statement: Orca currents
Identifiers: Canadiana (print) 20200176072 | Canadiana (ebook) 20200176080 |
ISBN 9781459826298 (softcover) | ISBN 9781459826304 (PDF) |
ISBN 9781459826311 (EPUB)
Classification: LCC PS8619.O975 J45 2020 | DDC jc813/.6—dc23

Library of Congress Control Number: 2020900530

Summary: In this high-interest accessible novel for middle readers,
fourteen-year-old Jenny is looking forward to her March break retreat.
But then she finds out that the boy who bullies her at school is going too.

Orca Book Publishers is committed to reducing the consumption of
nonrenewable resources in the making of our books. We make
every effort to use materials that support a sustainable future.

Orca Book Publishers gratefully acknowledges the support for its publishing
programs provided by the following agencies: the Government of Canada,
the Canada Council for the Arts and the Province of British Columbia
through the BC Arts Council and the Book Publishing Tax Credit.

Edited by Tanya Trafford
Design by Ella Collier
Cover artwork by gettyimages.ca/sodesignby
Author photo by Jay Parson

Printed and bound in Canada.

23 22 21 20 • 1 2 3 4

For some amazing kids—Marcus, Victoria, Mitchell, Elizabeth and Mackenzie

Chapter One

I peel back the lunch container's lid and admire the sandwich inside. Chicken salad with lettuce and tomato on a soft, buttery bun. I'm so glad Dad reminded me to add dill to the mayonnaise. I can smell the herb as soon as the lid is off. The sharp scent makes my taste buds tingle.

I pick up the sandwich. The ice packs in my bag have kept it chilled. Cool chicken salad is the perfect lunch for a surprisingly warm March day. I've been waiting all morning for a taste of this one. It's my last meal before I'm stuck eating camp food for the next nine days. I spent a long time making sure the sandwich would be perfect.

I lay the container next to me on the fountain's stone ledge. I hold the sandwich with two hands so I can take the biggest bite possible.

"Is that your lunch?"

I pause with the sandwich halfway to my mouth. My shoulders tense as I raise my eyes. I see a girl walking toward me. She's short and has a pixie haircut. She's also got purple braces on teeth too large for her otherwise small face. I lower the still-whole sandwich back to its container and give the girl a cautious smile.

"Yeah, it is," I say, nodding. I don't usually eat out in the open where everyone can see me. It's too easy for people like Austin Parks and his friends to make mean comments with every bite I take. But for the entire week of March break, I'll be part of the Granite County Young Leaders Retreat. Which means I've got no choice but to eat with others nearby.

I thought I could enjoy one final meal in peace though. The other kids are waiting across the park at the spot where the bus will pick us up. I thought I would be safe eating my sandwich in private before joining them.

I study the girl as she approaches. It doesn't seem as if she's about to call me names.

"That looks like a good sandwich," she says, plopping herself down on the ledge beside me. "My sister drove me out here. She wanted coffee, which meant my lunch consisted of hot chocolate and a stale muffin." She laughs.

"That sucks," I say, picking up the sandwich again. "I never eat fast food unless it comes from a truck."

"Those don't sound like very high standards," she says.

3

I smile. "A food truck, I mean. You know those trucks that have full kitchens installed in them? My dad's the chef of one called The Hungry Pup."

"I'm jealous," the girl says. "My dad can't cook anything if it doesn't come from the freezer. My mom's not much better. Did he make that for you?"

I can feel my cheeks warming. "No," I say, staring down at the bun. "He taught me the recipe, but I made this myself."

The girl laughs again. When I look up, she's leaning as far back as she can without falling into the fountain. She closes her eyes and turns her face toward the bright sun. "Now I'm even more jealous. I'd love to be able to cook," she says.

"Cooking's not hard," I say. I wonder how old the girl is. This retreat is for eighth and ninth graders from around the region. I wonder if she is fourteen like me or younger. I wonder if this is her first time too.

"I guess I wouldn't know," she says. "I've never bothered to try." She opens her eyes again and gives me a smile. "I'm Sarah, by the way."

"I'm Jenny," I tell her. It feels almost like a lie. I'm so used to my nickname, it's weird to hear my real name spoken aloud. Even if I'm the one saying it.

Sarah eyes my chicken salad again and then goes back to sunbathing.

"I hope you enjoy your sandwich," she says. "One of us should get a good meal today."

While Sarah's distracted by the sun, I bring the sandwich to my mouth. My teeth bite through the soft bun and the still-crunchy lettuce. When I taste the dilly chicken, my eyes flutter closed with delight.

Even with my eyes closed, I notice the shadow cutting across the sun as someone walks around the fountain.

"Well, look who it is," a familiar, awful voice says.

I swallow quickly. My delicious bite of sandwich slides down my throat like a stone.

I open my eyes to see the person I like least in the world standing before me. Austin Parks. He smirks, his cold blue eyes staring out from under his messy brown hair. I notice he's wearing a yellow Young Leaders T-shirt. My stomach churns.

"Enjoying your food, J.R.?" he asks.

I swallow again. This time I don't enjoy the lingering dilly taste of my sandwich at all.

Chapter Two

Hardly anyone calls me Jenny. Not since I got my nickname when I was eleven. And all because of that jerk Austin Parks.

We were in the same science class, and we got put together for a project. I was wearing a new sweater. It had brown, red and white stripes.

Austin had looked me up and down. Then he'd grinned and pointed at my stomach. "I think your parents gave you the wrong name. Jenny Royce? You look more like a *Jelly Roll* to me."

His friends had thought it was hilarious. I never wore that sweater again. But the new nickname stuck. Before that moment, Austin had never paid me much attention. After he'd invented the name, he made sure he used it more than anyone else.

"Aren't you going to say hello, J.R.?" Austin asks now. If teachers or people he doesn't know are nearby, Austin never says my nickname outright. It's always J.R. The rest of the time, Austin never calls me anything but Jelly Roll.

I put the rest of my sandwich back in the container and keep my head lowered as I blink back tears. I was really looking forward to this week. But now I wish I was already on my way home.

Of all the kids from school who could have shown up for this retreat, why does it have to be Austin standing here? He's the worst kind of person to be given a leadership role. He's mean and rude. He's useless.

Okay, that's not totally true. Austin's smart when he wants to be. He gets good grades, and last year he was on the school's math team. And I suppose he is a leader of sorts at school. He got a bunch of our classmates to start teasing me, didn't he? Even the ones who were supposed to be my friends.

I guess Austin has many talents. Above everything else, his greatest skill is making me miserable.

I wipe a tear away with the back of my hand. I have two rules when it comes to Austin Parks. One is that I never let him see me cry. I stare at my lap, hoping he will give up on teasing me. I never respond to Austin's taunts either. That's rule number two.

He stands in front of me. He is so close I can see his black sneakers even though I'm staring hard at my faded blue jeans. He wants me to say something.

But I stay silent like always, waiting for him to get bored. Today it doesn't take long. Ten seconds pass before he kicks the duffel bag that's on the ground next to my feet.

"Mouth must be too full to speak," he mumbles. I raise my head and he's still looking at me even as he turns to leave. "See you around, J.R.," he says. "I thought this retreat was going to suck. Now I think I might have some fun here after all."

He smiles as he walks away. I do my best not to let on how much his smug expression bothers me.

"Do you know that kid?" Sarah asks when Austin is out of earshot. She's been so quiet I almost forgot she was beside me.

"He goes to my school." I sigh. "I never would have come if I'd thought there was even a chance he'd be here."

"Yeah, he seems like a real loser." Sarah stands. She looks across the park to where several kids in yellow shirts are lining up. "Hey, come on. That's our ride," she says, pointing to the school bus pulling up against the curb.

"You go ahead. I'm going to finish my lunch," I say.

"Okay!" Sarah gives me a little wave and bounds off to join the group. She's quick. I'm glad I didn't go with her. She'd have left me behind in a few steps.

I wait for Sarah to reach the other kids, and then I walk over to the nearest trash can. Tears sting my eyes again. I wipe them away and dump the sandwich, only a single bite taken out of it, into the bin. I don't feel like eating anymore. My appetite vanished the moment I realized Austin would be tormenting me the entire time we're at this retreat.

I shove the empty sandwich container into my backpack and grab my duffel bag. As I cross the park, I count the kids lining up by the curb. If I'm the last one to arrive, it means there must be twenty of us in total.

One of the counselors is already talking when I sneak into the group. She uses a water bottle to point at the bus as she tells us it's time to board. I step next to Sarah.

"It'll take about half an hour to reach the camp," she says, filling me in on what I missed. "When we get there, we'll get our cabin, dump our bags and then have orientation." She grabs my arm and turns toward the bus. "Come on, let's board first so we can sit near the back."

I have to jog to keep up with her but manage to get ahead of everyone else. We give another counselor our names as we step onto the bus. Then we sit together in one of the back rows. When Austin gets on, I turn my whole body toward Sarah so I can look at her instead of him.

"Ignore him," Sarah says. "Otherwise it's going to be a long week."

"Yeah, you're right," I say. I face forward again and try to look cheerful.

As the bus doors shut and the driver switches on the engine, Austin looks over his shoulder. His eyes find mine, and his lips start to move. He's mouthing a secret meant just for me. I stare ahead and pretend I don't see what he's saying. Even though I do.

Jelly Roll.

I can't ignore Austin. I've spent years trying. It doesn't work. Which means Sarah is right.

This is going to be a long week.

Chapter Three

There are four girls in my cabin. I'm nervous about being in such close quarters with girls I don't know, but at least Sarah is rooming with me.

I meet the other two girls when we are given a few minutes to drop off our bags. Meera is tall and thin, with thick dark hair braided halfway down her back. Katrina is short with curly brown hair and splotchy skin. She's plump too. Like me.

Katrina and Meera seem nice. It's a relief to know they won't be teasing me. When you're used to being picked on, everyone you meet is a potential enemy.

"It's not as bad as I thought it would be," Katrina says when we step inside the cabin. The room is a small square. Two sets of bunk beds stand against opposite walls. It could do with a paint job, but at least the mattresses look pretty new.

"The camp I went to over winter break was a disaster," Meera says. "There was dirt everywhere, and the beds were like rocks." She flips her braid over one shoulder. "Anyone mind if I sleep up top?" She glances at each of us before she nabs one of the upper bunks.

"I'll take a bottom bunk," Katrina says. "I hate bunk beds. I roll in my sleep."

Sarah laughs. "Jenny, do you mind if I take the other upper bunk?" she asks. I'm glad she didn't start calling me J.R. after hearing Austin use it. It's nice to hear her saying my actual name.

"Yeah, that's fine," I say with a nod. I walk over and sit down on the last available bed.

"So," Sarah says after she's thrown her bags on the bunk above mine, "what do you think our leadership project will be? Last year we had to volunteer at a daycare. It was horrible. Me and little kids don't mix." I guess Sarah has been here before. She must be the same age as me.

"I would have loved that," Katrina says with a smile. "But the theme this year is 'locally grown.' I doubt that means locally grown humans."

"I hope not." Sarah's laugh comes out as a snort. "Maybe we'll help out on a farm or something. That'd be cool."

"As long as you don't mind getting dirty," I say.

My dad's the one who really wanted me to join this retreat. He thinks I have it in me to be a leader, if I can work on my confidence. He doesn't know about Austin or my nickname. I don't want to make him or my mom upset by telling them the truth. It wasn't until I discovered what the theme for the retreat was that I decided to come though. My dad uses local ingredients in his food truck. I thought it would be neat to work on my leadership skills and learn more about local food sources at the same time. I don't mind getting dirty. Going to a farm would be a lot of fun.

"As long as our project doesn't involve lizards or snakes, I'm good," Meera says.

"Do you think we'll get to work with the boys?" Katrina asks. I can practically see her cheeks turning pink. "Some of them are really cute."

"And at least one of them is a real loser," Sarah says.

Katrina looks intrigued. "Who?"

"We should probably get going," I blurt. Sarah gives me a confused glance, but I pretend not to notice. I don't want her telling the others about Austin. I don't want anyone else to know Austin and me are anything other than total strangers.

"Jenny's right. We should get ready for the tour," Sarah agrees at last.

Katrina walks to the door, and Meera follows behind her. I hang back so I can walk out with Sarah.

"Thank you," I whisper when we're the only ones left in the cabin. "I don't want anyone to know Austin and I know each other."

Sarah gives me a sideways stare. "You're welcome," she says. "But you shouldn't let him bug you so much."

"Yeah, I know," I say.

Sarah claps me on the shoulder before she leaves the cabin. I act like I forgot something in my bag so I can be alone. Sarah means well, but she doesn't understand what it's like to have someone like Austin around. There's no point in trying to explain it. It's easier to let her believe I'll take her advice. As if I could just stop feeling so embarrassed every time he's nearby.

I take a moment to settle my nerves. Then I walk out to join her and the others waiting for me.

Chapter Four

Orientation takes about an hour. We get a tour of the grounds and meet the staff members who will be running the retreat. Then we get our schedule. Most of each day will be spent on our leadership project. We'll also have themed activities and free time. Even though we're only here for a week, there are a lot of activities to choose from. If I'm careful, I can make sure Austin doesn't do any of the things I do. The less time we spend together, the better.

After our tour we go to the dining hall for dinner. We're served stale sandwiches and lukewarm tomato soup. I seriously regret throwing away my chicken salad. I should have kept it in its container. I would have gladly eaten it instead of this bland ham-and-cheese sandwich.

"Did they stockpile bread from last summer or something?" Sarah asks. She pulls apart her sandwich and eats the slice of ham.

"You can dip it in the soup to soften it up," Meera says. She hasn't eaten anything. Her meal has been pushed to the side. Instead she's reading the guidelines for our leadership project.

Katrina isn't eating either. Her arms are folded on the table, and she keeps staring across the room at a boy with shaggy blond hair. Every time he looks back at Katrina, her whole face goes pink.

"Okay, here are the rules for our project," Meera says. She glances up from her sheet to see if we are listening. We already heard this in orientation. But I give Katrina a nudge, and we both focus on Meera anyway.

"The counselors said they would answer questions about the project tomorrow when they post who is on which team," Sarah reminds her.

"Yes, but I want to make sure I have time to come up with questions," Meera replies. "Where was I? Oh yeah. It looks like this year's project will take place at a farmers' market. Each team will be in charge of designing a stall to showcase or promote local food sources."

"But we're not farmers," Katrina says.

"We don't have to sell food," Meera says. "We just need to showcase local foods in some way. How we do it is completely up to us."

"I hate that," Sarah says. "How are we supposed

to come up with an idea when our only guideline is that we can do whatever we want?"

"I think we're supposed to be creative," I offer.

"Yeah, but we only have eight full days after tonight. And at least half of that has got to be preparation time."

"We need to have our ideas ready by Tuesday," Meera says. She runs a finger along the page as she reads. Her green nail polish stands out against the white page and its black text. "And whatever we decide, we have to charge money for it."

"My cousin does tarot readings," Katrina says. "She'd be great at a market!"

"Are her tarot cards themed like food products?" Sarah asks.

"No," Katrina mumbles. She looks down at her soup bowl. Then she tenses. Her cheeks start to turn pink again. But this time it's not because of the blond-haired boy.

"What's wrong?" I ask as she glances over her shoulder.

Katrina shakes her head. "Nothing." She faces forward and changes the subject. "So we'll be in five teams of four, right?" she asks Meera.

"Yes, that's right," Meera says, nodding. "Each team will have a budget and access to some supplies for free."

"And the money we raise goes to the food bank," Katrina says. Her back stiffens again, but she doesn't look behind her. "Is that correct?"

"Yes, that's right," Meera says again.

"Well, it's better than taking care of snotty-nosed kids all day," Sarah says.

"You never know. Your group could decide to sell vegetable-shaped toys or something," I say with a smile.

Sarah laughs. "This bunch isn't up to building their own toys. I think I'm safe from having to play one of Santa's elves."

"Yes," Meera muses, "but you could set up healthy-snack sessions. Tell parents how they can use local foods for snacks and have the kids help make a snack to take with them."

"That's a great idea, Meera!" Katrina says.

Meera smiles. "It could work." I can tell she's already planning the details in her mind. She even grabs the notebook she brought with her. She jots down a few notes.

Sarah makes a face. "I hope we're not on the same team," she groans.

A sniggering noise catches my attention. A few seconds after it begins, something hits my back. I look down at the floor by my feet and see a balled-up piece of bread. There are several other balls of bread nearby. Ones that must have hit Katrina. No wonder she's been acting so strange.

I raise my eyes to the table of boys behind us.

Four of the boys I don't know. One of them I do. Austin meets my gaze. With a laugh he speaks to one of his new friends.

"Nice throw," he says, "but next time try a target that's not so hard to miss!"

Now it's my turn to blush. Even at a retreat meant to teach us about community spirit and cooperation, it has taken only one afternoon for Austin to turn some of the boys here into bullies.

My face is hot as I turn back around and try to act like nothing is wrong. But it's too late. Meera and Sarah, sitting across from Katrina and me, both heard what Austin said.

"Boys are so immature," Sarah says, scowling.

Meera shakes her head before returning to her notes.

"It's no big deal," I mutter. I glance down at my mostly untouched dinner. I pick up my spoon, then lower it back to the bowl.

Sarah looks at Katrina and me. Then she looks down at her own soup bowl.

"Well, this is too cold to eat anyway," she says. She removes her spoon and stands up. My eyes go wide as she picks up the bowl and starts to leave the table.

"Sarah, don't," I warn.

She doesn't listen. She walks toward the table of boys, and I stare down at my dinner. I don't want to watch what she's about to do. If anything happens and Austin thinks I was involved...

"Looking to get a second helping?"

Katrina and I both swivel around at the sound of a counselor speaking. Sarah is frozen in place behind Austin, her bowl raised above his head. She must have circled around the table and snuck up on him from behind. Part of me is sad her prank has been interrupted. Why should the counselor stop Sarah from humiliating Austin? No one stopped Austin from humiliating Katrina and me. Still, I'm relieved Sarah didn't get to go through with her plan.

I wouldn't want her getting kicked out of here on our first day.

"Just thought I'd see if anyone wanted my leftovers," Sarah says brightly. She gives the counselor a wide smile. Then she returns to our table with the bowl still in hand.

Austin glares at me. I turn away. I try not to grin at Sarah as she returns. That was pretty awesome. Even if I really wish she hadn't done it.

"That was almost brilliant," Meera says.

Sarah smirks and shrugs her shoulders. "There's plenty of time left in the week," she says.

I sigh, pushing my dinner away from me. The metallic smell of canned soup is making me feel sick. It doesn't even matter that Sarah didn't get to pour her soup over Austin's head. The fact that she tried makes my knees tremble under the table.

It's our first night here, and Austin is already annoyed with me. How can I make him forget I exist if my cabinmate won't let him do what he wants?

I am envious of her bravery. But I am worried she is going to end up getting me more than a few angry stares.

Chapter Five

I go straight back to the cabin after dinner is over. We have free time, but I don't want to risk any more incidents involving Austin or his gang.

The others return fairly soon after I do. Sarah complains that there are too many bugs out for March. She reeks of bug spray. Meera says she wants to work on her snack-stall idea. Katrina says there is no point in staying out when everyone else is inside.

Before long we are all talking about our projects again.

"How much money do you think we will raise?" Katrina asks. She sits cross-legged on her bunk, braiding her curly hair. But it's a challenge. With each twist of the braid, at least one or two curls escape.

"Depends on what you end up doing for your stall," Sarah says. She paces the small space between the bunks.

"But what if we only raise, like, fifty bucks?" Katrina asks. "What if we don't make enough money?"

I shrug. "Any amount helps. A food bank can do a lot with fifty dollars."

"Yeah, I suppose so," Katrina agrees. She finishes with her hair and sits back against her headboard.

"If I get overruled," Meera says from her top bunk, "will one of you use my idea? I'm working too hard for it not to be used." She has her phone out. She has been looking up snack recipes since she got back to the cabin.

"You never know, we could all be on the same team," I say.

Katrina smiles. "That would be nice."

"Yeah, but it's not very likely, is it?" Sarah says. She stops pacing and puts her hands on the hips of her pink pajama pants. "They will probably want us to mingle with the other kids."

I sigh. She is right, but I wish she weren't. Sarah doesn't want to work on this project with Meera. But I think this whole week would be a lot easier if the four of us were all on the same team.

"Working with some of the boys would be nice too," Katrina says with a smile.

Sarah starts pacing again. She stops after only a couple of turns. "I can't focus on the project," she exclaims. "I'm too hungry."

"No kidding," I say, thinking of our disappointing dinner.

"There's a grocery store down the road," Katrina says. "I saw it on the way here. Tomorrow I'm going to get some snacks, if I can figure out how to get back there."

"That's fine for tomorrow," Sarah says, "but what about right now?"

"We could sneak into the kitchen," Meera suggests. She puts away her phone and climbs down from her bunk. "Lots of food in there."

"What if we get caught?" Katrina asks.

Sarah scoffs. "Who cares about getting caught? The more important question is, what would we eat? We all had the food. It wasn't exactly awe-inspiring."

I bite my lip and look around at my cabinmates. "Well," I say slowly, "I could make us something."

"Ooh, yes!" Sarah claps her hands together as she hurries to the door. She grabs a flashlight from the window ledge and shoves her bare feet into her sneakers. Then she turns back to wait for the rest of us.

"You cook?" Meera asks.

My heart is pounding. I have never offered to cook for anyone but my family before. I never expected I would be cooking at the Young Leaders Retreat.

"She is great," Sarah says before I can respond. "You should have seen her lunch."

I get up and throw a sweater on over my T-shirt. Not that I'll need it. My face is so hot from embarrassment that a snowstorm would feel like a warm summer breeze.

"I doubt they will have the ingredients for chicken salad, but I'm sure I can come up with something," I say. My face cools down. I love cooking, and I like these girls. This will be fun.

Meera smiles. "Great!"

She and Sarah lead the way, and Katrina trails behind me. We sneak out into the night, following the path from our cabin. We don't have to worry too much about being seen. There is no one around. The counselors must not be concerned about us breaking the curfew rule. Either that or they are over keeping an eye on the boys' cabins.

It is easy to make it around the well-lit campground. We pass an empty beach and cross over a wide expanse of lawn to reach the dining hall. We don't see a single person. I'm a bit disappointed. I had imagined rebellion would be more thrilling.

The dining hall is locked. Meera pulls a bobby pin out of her braid. She snaps it in two and uses it as a pick.

"My parents have sent me to camp every summer and winter since I was four," she tells us. She holds one half of the pin in place at the top of the keyhole. "Can't say I haven't learned some useful skills along the way!" She pushes the second half into the bottom part of the lock and carefully turns it back and forth. It takes only a couple of jiggles before the lock unlatches.

Meera pushes open the wooden door and slips the pins into her pocket. She acts like it is no big deal.

I'm impressed by how easy she made it look. I'm also curious to know how many other locks she has picked over the years.

"You have to teach me that," Sarah says as we step into the dark dining hall.

Meera nods. "Later. For now, let's eat."

Chapter Six

"Do you think they will notice the missing food?" Katrina asks.

"Not if we clean up," Meera replies as we walk into the kitchen. "If they don't suspect anyone has been here, they won't be on the lookout for missing items. And if they do notice, they will probably think they miscounted."

"Besides, if we do get caught, we can tell them we were practicing our leadership skills," Sarah adds. She hops onto the prep counter. "You know, taking charge to eliminate our unnecessary hunger." She keeps her flashlight on so we don't have to turn on the main lights. "The worst they will do is put us on kitchen duty. If they let Jenny cook, that might not be much of a punishment anyway."

Sarah's comment catches me off guard. I laugh so hard I double over. "You have never even tasted my cooking!" I say. "You only saw my sandwich and said it *looked* good."

"Oh, it tasted good too," Sarah says. "I could tell. And the faster you cook something now, the faster I can prove I know what I'm talking about."

There is not a lot to choose from in the kitchen. But I do find stuff to make pancakes. I whisk the dry ingredients. Meera cracks in an egg while I add milk and melted butter. Sarah slices some bruised peaches we got from the walk-in fridge into a bowl. I cover the fruit with butter and cinnamon. Then I spoon it onto the hot griddle next to the bubbling pancake batter. When the pancakes are done, I load up the plates Meera set out and then top them with the cooked fruit. I squirt a bit of canned whipped cream on each pile and drizzle syrup over everything.

Everyone digs in, standing right there at the counter. No one says anything for a few mouthfuls. Then Katrina declares, "These are the best pancakes I have ever eaten!" She licks whipped cream from her fork.

"Told you I knew what I was talking about," Sarah says with her mouth full of peach and pancake.

I shrug, trying not to feel too pleased. "It would be better with real cream and proper maple syrup," I say.

Meera shakes her head. "No, it's great," she says. "Much better than what we ate for dinner. The others would be super jealous if they knew what we were doing. They would probably even be willing to pay you for this meal."

"Hey, that's an idea," Sarah says as she picks a bit of peach from her braces. "You should cook at the farmers' market. People always want to nibble while they're shopping."

"What?" I take a step backward and nearly burn my arm on the still-hot griddle. "No. I don't cook in front of people."

"You cooked in front of us," Katrina says.

"That's different," I say.

"Why don't you want to cook in front of other people?" Sarah asks.

I shrug my shoulders again and turn to start taking dishes to the sink. People tease me enough about my size without knowing how much I love cooking. I like the way I look. And I love the food I create. But it would be too easy to make fun of the big girl who feels most at home in the kitchen. I don't want to be shamed about something I enjoy doing.

"Come on, let's get these cleaned so we can get back to our cabin," I say instead. The other girls are quiet for a minute. I can picture them sharing glances behind my back. But then they start helping me with the dishes. With four of us working, it doesn't take long before everything is back where it belongs.

The kitchen has a rear exit that will lock behind us when we leave. But first we head back into the dining hall so we can lock the main door from the inside. As we pass one of the tables, Meera stops. She looks at something on the tabletop that we didn't notice on our way in.

"What's this?" she asks. She snatches up the paper.

"It's the list of teams," Sarah says. She stands on her toes to look over Meera's shoulder. "Bonus! A good meal and early access to the list. Are we in the same group, Meera?"

"No, doesn't look like any of us are together," Meera says. She passes the list to Sarah. Sarah reads it over and passes it to Katrina. When she's done she hands the paper to me.

"At least I don't have to worry about making snacks for little kids," Sarah says, giving Meera a playful punch on the shoulder.

"There aren't any boys on my team," Katrina says with a sigh. "Do you think they would let us switch?"

"I doubt it," I say.

I search for my name, and my throat goes dry. I would gladly take Katrina's place. I would gladly switch with anyone. One other girl and two boys are on my team. And one of those boys is Austin Parks.

It almost looks like a mistake to see my real name listed on the sheet. Austin's going to hate being my teammate. It's not my fault the counselors put us together. But he is going to blame me for it anyway. Which means that after tomorrow, no one is going to know who Jenny Royce is anymore.

My name might as well be listed as Jelly Roll.

Chapter Seven

I don't want to go to breakfast in the morning.
I want to lie in bed all day and pretend I never
saw the teams list. But I'm hungry. If I don't eat
something, my stomach will grumble all morning.
I will probably get a headache too. Austin already
gave me a restless night. I'm not going to let him
cause me an aching head as well.

"You will never guess what we're having for breakfast," Meera says when I reach the dining hall. I'm the last one from our cabin to get there. I was the first to wake up this morning, but I was so slow that the others went ahead without me.

"Leftover sandwiches from yesterday's dinner?" I ask through a yawn.

"No." Meera smiles. "Pancakes."

I look at her in surprise, and then we both start laughing. I wonder if pancakes were always on the menu for today or if a lingering smell in the kitchen inspired the chef.

This morning's pancakes are soggy and bland. I would be complaining along with everyone else if it weren't for the looks I keep sharing with my cabinmates. I nearly snort milk out my nose watching Sarah's frown as she takes bite after disappointing bite.

Sharing a delicious secret with my new friends

makes me feel a lot better. But once breakfast is over, the morning takes a turn for the worse.

We go outside and separate into our teams. I guess Austin didn't bother to check the list ahead of time. I can see the disgust on his face as soon as he realizes we will be working together.

He waits quietly while a girl named Audrey and a boy named Ollie join us. Audrey is pretty. She twirls her shining brown hair around her finger as she walks toward us. At least Ollie wasn't one of the boys hanging out with Austin last night. He's wearing silver sunglasses that stand out against his dark hair. He holds out his hand for me to shake when we are introduced.

"So what are we going to do for our project?" Audrey asks. She loops her thumbs into the pockets of her jeans.

"Time to start planning," Ollie says. "But we should get some paper and pencils so we can write everything down before we forget."

I smile at Ollie. He would have made a good partner for Meera.

"No need. I already have an idea," Austin says.

Ollie looks at him, but it's hard to read his expression through his sunglasses.

"We could each present an idea and then all vote on the best one," I offer. I try to sound like I'm not worried how Austin will react. But when he turns his gaze on me, I can't help flinching. His blue eyes are narrowed, and his mouth twitches.

"No point," Austin says. He talks slowly, making sure I catch every word. "I can already say that no one will like your idea. Who would pay to watch a one-person pie-eating contest?"

My cheeks burn, and I bite my lip to try to keep the tears from forming. Rule number one. No crying allowed. Audrey acts like her flip-flops have suddenly become extremely interesting. "That…is not…" I stammer. But then I look down at my shoes too. "Never mind." There is no point in arguing. I know how this goes.

"So what is your big idea then, Austin?" Ollie asks. It may be hard to read his face, but the annoyed tone of Ollie's voice is easy enough to understand. He crosses his arms over his chest and stares at Austin. I like the way Austin squirms under the attention.

"We'll set up a game," Austin says. The first words out of his mouth are quiet, but as he talks, his confidence returns. "You know, like an apple-bobbing game or something."

"I love bobbing for apples," Audrey says with a big smile.

Her words sound fake. I can't believe it. She's flirting with Austin! Gross.

"How is that in keeping with our theme?" Ollie asks. He sounds unimpressed by Austin's idea. I'm unimpressed by it too.

"I don't know—we'll use local apples," Austin says with a roll of his eyes.

"I'm not sure that's a good idea," Ollie says. "I don't think anyone is going to pay to bob for apples at a farmers' market."

"Well, I think it's the best idea anyone is going to come up with, and I vote we do it," Austin says. He crosses his arms over his chest to match Ollie's stance. It makes him look every bit as menacing.

"I vote for it too," Audrey says. I gape at her. She gives me an uncertain look before smiling sweetly at Austin.

"Well, I vote against it," Ollie says. "And I would like to hear some other ideas."

Austin glares at him, but then he looks at me instead. "Two to one," he says, the mocking smirk I know so well creeping onto his lips. "Looks like you have the deciding vote, J.R. So what will it be? Are you voting for my idea? Or are you voting against it?"

The way he says it makes everything clear. If I vote against his idea now, I'll pay for it later.

I look at Ollie, and he looks at me. He is probably waiting for me to be sensible and vote down this terrible idea. I want to. But Ollie doesn't understand. Our week here just began. And even after March break is over, I will still have to deal with Austin's cruelty at school.

I give Ollie my best apologetic shrug. Then I look down at the ground.

"I vote for your idea, Austin," I say.

Ollie curses under his breath. He throws his hands in the air and storms away from us.

"That's what I thought," Austin says. He pats me on the head like I'm a dog. "Good choice, J.R."

He turns his back on me and whispers something to Audrey. They both laugh.

Chapter Eight

"Jenny, can I talk to you outside for a minute?"

I look up from my book to see Ollie standing beside me. I can tell from his voice that he is worried about something. It's not hard to guess what.

"Sure," I say.

Everyone is in the activities hall tonight. There is a table-tennis table and a whole closet full of board games to play. After this morning's disastrous team meeting, I decided to spend my night reading by the fire.

Now I get up from my cozy chair and follow Ollie outside. The dark sky is clear, but it is cold. I shiver as soon as we are out of the hall. I can see the fireplace through the window near where we stand. I wish I'd invited Ollie to sit next to me instead of coming out here.

"It's about our project," Ollie says once we are alone. As if I didn't already know.

"Austin's idea isn't great," I say.

Ollie sighs. "The idea sucks," he says. "But I wouldn't even care about that if we were actually working on it. We had three hours to plan out the project today, and we have nothing to show for it."

He is right. After we all agreed to his apple-bobbing idea, Austin spent the rest of our team session playing on his phone. After we were given our budget, Ollie tried to get some work done without him, but Austin would not allow it. He was quick to shoot down all of Ollie's ideas. And he gave me a warning look not to offer any suggestions of my own. It is now Sunday night, and we need show the counselors a solid plan by Tuesday.

"I know," I mumble. I peer through the window. I spot Austin playing table tennis with Audrey and her friends. From out here, he looks normal. Almost friendly. It's amazing how deceiving appearances can be.

"We have to do something," Ollie says. "I'm not here to play games. Next year I want to do an exchange program at school. I'm hoping to get a leadership reference from one of the counselors. But that won't happen if it's obvious we didn't put any effort into our stall."

Inside, Austin looks up from his game. I am startled when he looks right at me. His expression is blank. It makes me uneasy.

I look away from Austin's creepy stare. "Why don't you talk to Audrey?" I ask.

Ollie shakes his head. "She likes Austin. She won't go against him. I need your help, Jenny. *Please.*"

It is the second time he's used my real name. It makes me want to help.

"Well, what can I do?" I ask.

Ollie smiles. His hopeful expression makes me instantly regret saying anything.

"We can make the best of a bad idea. We can expand on it, create a supply list and plan out how it all might work," he says. "If we do it quietly, Austin won't know until it's too late."

"I'm not sure." If Austin finds out I was involved, it won't matter that I ever agreed with his idea. He will consider me a traitor. He will make my life more miserable than it already is.

"Please, Jenny," Ollie says. He steps close to me. In the glow of the window I can see his eyes. They are blue, like Austin's. But they are much softer. And much more kind. I want to help him. But I'm not sure it is worth suffering Austin's wrath to help a boy I don't even know.

When I don't respond, Ollie sighs again. "Just think about it, okay? Let's talk some more tomorrow after our meeting." He gives me one last look, then walks off into the night.

I watch him go, thinking about what he has suggested. If we are careful to keep it secret, his plan could work.

"Either you've found yourself a boyfriend, or you're plotting against me."

I whip my head around so fast my neck hurts. Austin is standing next to me. I didn't even hear him come outside.

"And since there is no way anyone would want to go out with you," he continues, "my bet is on the latter. So what was that conversation with Ollie all about, Jelly Roll?"

The nickname hits hard, even though I've heard it at least a hundred times before.

"We were just talking," I say. I cross my arms over my chest.

"About our project, right?" Austin asks.

I consider lying, but there is no point. Austin already knows the truth. There is nothing I could say to convince him he is wrong.

"Ollie wants us to succeed," I tell him. "He doesn't want to change your idea. He just wants to make sure everything goes as well as it can."

"Well, I don't," Austin says.

His response is so unexpected that I forget about being nervous. "What do you mean? You don't want the project to go well?" I ask.

"No, I don't," Austin says. I stare at him in confusion. After a few silent seconds, he shrugs. "My dad's new girlfriend thinks I'm not living up to my full potential. It wasn't my choice to come here. It was hers. I want them both to know they wasted their money sending me to this stupid retreat."

I'm surprised by his honesty. And by my desire to ask him more. But his hard stare is so icy, it makes me shiver from a different kind of cold. I don't say anything.

"We need to fail," he adds. "Which means you need to stop working so hard. Or maybe I will have to make a trip to the grocery store to stock up on snack foods. There's a sale on chocolate jelly rolls. I think everyone here would be happy to share them. Know what I mean?"

I get the idea. I nod. "Yeah."

Austin gives me a charming smile. It is somehow worse than his sneer.

"Good." He wipes his hands together as if brushing off invisible dirt. "Nice talking with you, Jelly Roll."

I don't watch as Austin walks away. I stare at my feet instead, thinking about the two conversations I just had. Ollie's concern makes sense, and I would like to help him out. And of course Austin is capable of making my life unbearable. But there is a part of me that is curious about what he said about his family. Did his dad's girlfriend really make him come here? Being forced to attend camp must suck. It almost makes me feel sorry for him.

Almost.

I go back inside the hall to get my book, and then I head back to the cabin for the night. I'm not in the mood for reading by the fire anymore. I want to curl up in my bunk and try to pretend it's almost time to go home.

Chapter Nine

"Your whole team is wasting time," Sarah says the next morning. I didn't tell anyone what happened last night. But Sarah saw Ollie and Austin talking to me. After she got back to the cabin, she spent the rest of the night bugging me about it. I haven't given her the details. But she has guessed that Austin's visit wasn't friendly.

"Austin doesn't want our help," I say. "He wants to control the whole project." I watch as Sarah paces the room. She's been annoyed since she woke up and heard the rain pattering outside. She was hoping it would be warm enough for a volleyball game this afternoon. But there is a storm on the way, and the temperature has dropped.

"That loser doesn't want to do anything more than he has to," she says. She scowls as she paces. She may be small, but she can be intimidating. "He will probably just throw some apples in a bucket."

If he does that much, I'll be impressed. Sarah doesn't know Austin is planning to make sure our project is a complete failure. It is kind of weird. I've seen Austin put a lot of effort into projects at school. Last year he got the highest mark of all the eighth graders on a history project about the Civil War. I'm used to him being mean. But I've never seen him intentionally fail before. I can't stop thinking about what he said about his dad and his dad's girlfriend. It must suck to be sent away like this.

"You should plan a backup," Meera suggests. She's sitting on her bunk and playing on her phone. Katrina is not here. She left the cabin early this morning. She didn't even come back after breakfast.

"That's right, you should," Sarah agrees. "That way, when he fails to plan anything, you can pull something together at the last minute. Besides, at least then the rest of you will have a project to work on."

"That's what Ollie wants to do," I admit. "But Austin would be furious if he found out we were working behind his back."

"So what?" Sarah asks. She stops and gives me a pointed stare. "Why are you so afraid of him?"

I pick up my book and focus on one of the pages. It's not just that my nickname makes me uncomfortable. Austin is capable of more than name calling. Last year someone painted *Jelly Roll* on my locker and shoved a whole bag of cake crumbs in through the slats. I never got proof of who did it, but I know it was him.

A lot of kids at school tease me. But Austin is the only one who has ever gone beyond simply calling me names. He is a total jerk. I can't believe I was actually feeling bad for him last night.

"Leave her alone, Sarah," Meera says.

I don't like the pity in her voice. I don't want the others to feel sorry for me. I just want them to ignore Austin and stop worrying about my team.

Sarah sighs. "Sorry, Jenny," she says. "I'm being a brat. I hate thunderstorms, and I'm starving. Breakfast was awful this morning."

"We can sneak back to the kitchen tonight," I say. I didn't feel like cooking last night. I don't really want to cook today either. But I already saw what is on the menu for dinner this evening. Sandwiches. Again.

"Really? That would be amazing," Sarah says. Her eyes light up. "Do you think they have any pasta? I would love a giant bowl of something cheesy."

"I'm sure we can find something for you," I say with a laugh. I like cooking for Sarah and the others. I am already thinking of three different dishes I could throw together.

I look out the cabin's small window. The rain is steady, but the storm hasn't reached the cabins yet. I slide off my bunk and grab my coat.

"What are you doing?" Sarah asks as I head for the door.

"I'm going to take a quick peek at the storeroom in the hall," I say. When I open the cabin door, I realize just how hard it is raining. But I still want to go out. "Breakfast is done, so no one will be around. I want to get an idea of what I can make tonight."

"Look for the noodles," Sarah says. Meera smiles at Sarah's remark and then looks back down at her phone.

"Got it," I say. I give them a wave before I step through the door.

It's pretty miserable outside. I pull up my hood and start jogging toward the dining hall. On the way I think about our project. I want to help Ollie, but I don't think I can go against Austin. I would rather feel guilty about getting Ollie's hopes up than live in constant fear, wondering how Austin might pay me back for undermining him. I wish I had been put in a group with someone like Sarah. She would refuse to let Austin bully anyone like this.

I cross the lawn and duck under the shelter of the dining hall's awning. I use the inside of my coat sleeve to wipe the rain from my face as I catch my breath. My stomach growls at the thought of going to the kitchen. Maybe while I'm inside I can sneak a few oranges or something to bring back to the cabin.

"What, you didn't get your fill at breakfast, fatty?"

My shoulders tense, and I spin around to face Austin. I recognize his voice. But no one is there. I turn in a circle, confused. Then I hear someone around the corner speak.

"I thought—I thought we were going to meet alone," a girl says. I recognize her voice too. Katrina.

I'm glad the rain is loud enough to cover the sound of my footsteps. When I look around the corner, I see Katrina leaning against the main door of the hall. Her head is lowered, and her arms are wrapped protectively across her stomach. Two boys stand across from her. One hangs awkwardly back, while the other one—Austin—presses in close.

"Wait, is that why you didn't want me to come with you?" Austin looks at his friend. I recognize the blond-haired boy Katrina was staring at during our first dinner here. Liam.

Liam looks at Katrina sheepishly. Austin starts to laugh.

"Going on a little date?" he asks.

Katrina looks up at him, mortified. The other boy stares down at the ground.

"We were just going to hang out," Katrina says. Her voice trembles when she says it. She glances at the other boy, but he keeps his eyes lowered.

"Yeah, right," Austin jeers. "Be careful when you kiss her, Liam. She might mistake you for a snack and try to eat you up."

The other boy's lips settle into an ugly sneer.

"Gross," he mutters.

Katrina's face falls even further. She looks like she is about to cry.

"Here's a tip," Austin says. He steps even closer to Katrina. "No one likes fat girls."

"Let's go," Liam says. He grabs Austin's shoulder and pulls him back. Austin's eyes linger on Katrina for a few long seconds before he walks off. Liam pauses for a moment like he is going to say something to Katrina. But he doesn't.

The boys walk off together, and Katrina collapses against the door. I watch her curl into a ball. But instead of running to comfort her, I turn and run around to the back of the dining hall.

The kitchen door is unlocked. I push my way inside and pull the door shut behind me. I burst into tears.

Chapter Ten

For once Austin is making fun of someone other than me. But I'm crying almost as hard as I did the day I had to spend two hours after school cleaning crumbs from my locker.

I stand next to the kitchen door as I sob. I'm shaking so hard even my teeth are chattering.

I have always been the one being teased. I have never watched it happen to someone else.

Is that what other people see when Austin calls me names?

I understand now why Sarah gets so angry when she hears I've given in to Austin's demands. I didn't think she understood what it's like to be made fun of. But maybe I was wrong. Maybe she gets so angry because she *does* know what it is like.

Because right now I'm angry. I'm sad and scared and worried about Katrina. But more than anything else, I'm angry.

I'm angry with Austin. I'm angry with the other boy who said nothing while a girl he likes was bullied. I'm angry with everyone who has ever stood by while the same thing happened to me. But mostly I'm angry with myself. I could have stepped in to defend Katrina, and I didn't. I didn't do anything because I was scared Austin would hurt me just like he was hurting her.

I look around the kitchen for some tissue I can use to dry my eyes. I think about Austin. I think about every time he has made me nervous or afraid. I think about every time I have held back tears so he wouldn't see me cry.

I find a roll of paper towel next to the sink. I tear off a piece and dab my eyes. Then I look around at the dark kitchen. I've always tried to hide my love of cooking because I knew it would give Austin ammunition. But I'm sick of planning my life around his attacks. I love food. And I love cooking.

The only thing I don't love is Austin's cruddy attitude.

I rest my elbows on the prep counter. After Austin started teasing me, I began to see the world differently. After what just happened to Katrina, I'm seeing things differently again. Looking at this kitchen laid out before me, I'm getting an idea.

For years I've given Austin and others like him so much power. Seeing Katrina crushed down has made me realize it is finally time to take some of that power back.

I spend the next half hour in the kitchen, walking and thinking. I drip rainwater everywhere. The staff will know someone has been in here when they start preparing for lunch. But I'm not worried. Finally I head into the dining hall to wait for the others to arrive for our daily team meeting.

By the time everyone starts rushing in out of the rain, I have a plan. My throat is dry as I wait for the members of my team to arrive. I swallow hard before I get up and make my way over to our table.

Ollie's sunglasses are on top of his head. I wonder briefly why he's even wearing them. He looks bored. His fingers tap a silent rhythm against his thigh as he watches Audrey putting up her wet hair. Austin is staring at his phone. None of them notice my approach.

"We're not doing apple bobbing at the farmers' market," I say in as firm a voice as I can muster. All three of them jump when I speak.

Austin is quick to recover. "I'm sorry, what did you say?" he asks. He gives me a nasty look.

My gut reaction is to turn away from him. But I force myself to stare into his eyes instead. It is something I've never done, and it is so unexpected it makes him twitch.

"We're not going with your idea, Austin," I repeat. My voice is steady despite how nervous I am. I walk closer to his seat so I can stand over him, big and tall and strong. "I take back my vote. And I'm making another suggestion." I glance at Audrey. Then I focus my attention on Ollie. "I think we should serve food," I say. "I can cook. I'm good with food."

Austin scoffs, but Ollie doesn't give him time to make a joke.

"That could work," he says. "What kind of food would we serve?" His expression has changed from bored to excited. His eagerness fuels my confidence.

"I was thinking we could do wraps," I tell him. "And pie rolls for dessert." I remember the joke Austin made about my one-person pie-eating contest. As mean as the joke was, it did give me the perfect idea for our menu. "We can make everything using local ingredients from the market vendors. And my dad owns a food truck," I say. "I'm sure he would let us use it for the day."

"I went to a food truck once that served the best turkey club," Audrey pipes up. She looks as enthusiastic as Ollie does. I'm surprised. I expected her to argue against my idea. Maybe she has realized how dull it is to sit around doing nothing on the project. Or maybe she is done flirting with Austin. Whatever it is, it's nice to have the support.

"A food truck would be awesome!" Ollie says.

I crouch down and rest my arms on the table. Then I look back at Austin. He is furious. I'm tempted to shy away from his angry expression. But I don't. I force myself to give him a hard, serious look.

"And the best part is, we've already got the name."

"Yeah, and what is that?" Austin asks. His voice is thin. Somehow I know he is trying to be tough but can't quite manage it.

"My dad's food truck is called The Hungry Pup," I explain. "There's a big cartoon dog on the side of it. He can be our mascot." I continue to stare at Austin until he begins to fidget in his seat. Then I let out a long breath. "We can call our stall Roll Over."

Chapter Eleven

I've known Austin Parks since we were both ten years old. In all that time, I've never seen him speechless.

Until now.

"Roll Over?" Ollie asks while Austin stares at me in silence. My heart is pounding. I'm terrified by Austin's look. But I'm also proud of making him look that way.

"It's kind of an inside joke," I say. I keep my eyes on Austin as I speak. Then I look at my other teammates again. Ollie is giving Austin a dark stare. Audrey is looking at me with a sympathetic smile. I've spilled Austin's secret. At least part of it. It is embarrassing. But it is also a relief. They know about his teasing. And I got to be the one to tell them.

"The name also ties in with the dog on the side of the truck," I add. "And that's where I got the idea for what kind of foods we can serve."

"Okay, I get it," Ollie says after a minute. He looks at me with a smile. I take a deep breath before smiling back.

"My dad makes pie rolls in his truck. Handheld desserts perfect for shoppers wanting to eat on the go. And our wraps are rolls too, when you think of it."

"Sounds good to me!" says Audrey. "Are you going to do all the cooking?"

"Yes." I move around the table and sit between her and Ollie. Austin is across from me. He still looks shocked. "Making wraps is just like making sandwiches. And I've been baking pie rolls with my parents since I was little."

"Do you really think we can pull this off?" Audrey asks. "We've only got a few days."

I nod. "It will be tight. But if we get organized and make a plan, we can prep some of the things ahead of time. We should be okay. But we need to make sure there is an onsite kitchen at the market where we can store everything until we bring it into the truck."

"We can talk to the counselors about it," Ollie says. "They'll know the layout of the building."

"I'll work on some signs," Audrey says with a grin. "If we need to, we can ask the market vendors for spare cardboard."

"Hold on," Ollie says. He stands up. "I'll grab a notebook from one of the other teams. We need to start writing this all down."

Ollie leaves, and Audrey turns to Austin.

"Do you want to help me with the signs?" she asks.

He doesn't even look at her. His eyes are trained on me. I'm sure he is planning his revenge, and I would be lying if I said it didn't frighten me. But I can't focus on that. Right now I'm working on our project. I'm taking on the leadership role I came to this retreat to develop.

"Austin is not going to help," I tell Audrey. She looks back and forth between us. Then she pulls out her ponytail and busies herself with putting it up again. Austin continues to stare at me, saying nothing.

When Ollie returns we spend the next hour planning. We write out different menu options. I also show Audrey a picture of my dad's truck so she can copy the cartoon dog onto our signs. It feels good to be productive. It doesn't even matter if we are a day behind the other teams. We're working now. And we're putting together something that is going to be great.

When the team sessions end, we have everything outlined. Audrey is excited to start painting the signs.

Ollie is going to figure out how we can get the best prices on the ingredients we need so we can stay within our budget.

Austin never leaves the table. He doesn't pitch in any ideas or even make fun of the ones we toss around. He doesn't say anything. He just sits there, never taking his eyes off me. It's awful. But I survive it without needing to run away or pretend I'm someplace else.

He stays until the last. And so do I. I'm not sure why I don't leave when the others do. I could get up and walk away before Austin has a chance to get me alone. But I don't want to imagine what he might have said to me. I would rather know it firsthand.

I gather the papers I've scribbled on. Then I glance at Austin. As always, he looks cold and mean. But he also looks a bit broken. Which could be dangerous.

"Bad choice, Jelly Roll," he says.

For a moment I don't respond. But this time it's not out of fear. There are a million things I could say to Austin right now. I just don't want to waste any more of my time on this boy.

"*Good choice,*" I counter. I stand up and walk past him on my way out of the dining hall. I notice that his fists are clenched so tight his knuckles have turned white.

Chapter Twelve

"This place is awesome," Sarah says. Her legs dangle over the edge of the small counter inside my dad's food truck. I shoo her off. Her sandals smack loudly against the floor as she hops down.

I place a tray of uncooked blueberry pie rolls on the counter. "It's a bit cramped," I say with a grin. "But I love it in here."

"Your dad really doesn't mind lending it to us for the farmers' market?" she asks. She hands me a carton of eggs, and I grab a fork from a nearby drawer.

"The Hungry Pup is only open during the day on Thursdays, Fridays and Saturdays. It's fine for us to use it tomorrow." It is Saturday night. My parents drove the truck up here a couple of hours ago. Tomorrow is the day of the farmers' market, and then the Young Leaders retreat will be over.

I'm excited to go home. I want to sleep in my own bed and cook in my own kitchen. But it has been a lot of fun planning our food. I am excited about tomorrow, but I'm still worried about Austin. Since we changed our plans, the only thing he's done is sulk. I wish I could enjoy the peace. I'm worried it is the calm before the storm.

"We're here!"

Sarah and I both look to the door as Meera and Katrina carry in a big cooler. Ollie comes in after them with a second cooler of his own. My cabinmates didn't need to help us set everything up, but I'm happy they offered. It's good to have extra help—especially since a member of our team isn't helping at all. It's also nice to have company while I'm working. It's actually kind of fun having others nearby to watch me create.

"Great. Put the coolers there, and we can start packing up the pie rolls." I point to a free bit of counter near the fridge. Sarah helps with the packing, while I get to work crimping the edges of the pie crusts.

"How are we doing?" Ollie asks as he lowers a tray of peach pie rolls into his cooler. We weren't able to find all fresh ingredients. But some of the vendors had frozen fruit from last season's crop, so we have managed to get a nice selection of fillings. We have toppings for the wraps as well. We made some of them earlier today. The rest we'll make tomorrow morning.

"I think we are pretty much finished," I tell him. "These blueberry pie rolls are almost ready to go in the oven. The wraps are packed up. All that's left are the apple pie rolls. I'll make those tonight before I go to bed."

"Then I guess we're all set," he says. "Audrey is already finished her signs. We'll take the supplies into the market soon."

The farmers' market is close to the campground we're staying at for the retreat. We'll store our food in the building's staff kitchen overnight.

"I can't believe it's all working out." Ollie smiles. "I'm so glad you changed your mind."

"Why *did* you change your mind anyway?" Sarah asks. "I mean, it's a good thing you did. But what happened?"

I look quickly at Katrina. She has been keeping to herself since the incident earlier this week. As far as I know, she hasn't told anyone what happened. I didn't tell her I saw it, but that evening when we were all getting ready for bed, I went over to her bunk. When no one else was nearby I whispered, "It's going to be okay, Katrina."

She looked at me and then turned to face the wall. But I think she knew what I meant. If she ever wants to talk, I hope she knows she can count on me to listen.

"I saw things from a different perspective," I say with a shrug. I finish crimping the pies rolls and start brushing the crusts with egg so they will be golden once they are baked. "Austin has ruined enough. I couldn't let him ruin this too."

"Do you think he'll help out tomorrow?" Meera asks.

Ollie and I exchange glances.

"I doubt it," Ollie says. "I'd be surprised if he even sticks around. It wouldn't be hard for him to sneak away and blow off the whole farmers' market."

Austin wants to fail. If the counselors see that he is absent tomorrow, he won't pass. Maybe he will get his wish and never have to come back. I don't really care.

"So he'll go through the whole week without doing any work?" Katrina asks. "It's not fair. People like him, they shouldn't get their way. But they always do."

"Not always," I say. "People like Austin have their reasons for being jerks. They're not good reasons, but they are reasons. They try to control others to make up for what they can't control themselves." I finish brushing the pie crusts and smile up at Katrina. "It's his problem, not ours," I say.

Katrina eyes me carefully. By the way her face brightens as she nods, I think she understands.

Chapter Thirteen

I stay up late making pies.

The camp's kitchen is quiet after curfew. The counselors gave me special permission to finish baking before I go to bed. I even have a proper key to lock up when I'm done.

I set out my ingredients for the apple pie rolls. These are my favorites. Buttery puffs of pastry with gooey, sweet apple filling. I might have to taste-test one of them once they're baked. Maybe two.

I start blending the butter and flour for the pastry. When I hear the kitchen door open, I don't even look up from my bowl.

"You're supposed to be in your cabin," I say, thinking it's Sarah or Ollie. When no one answers, I raise my head.

Austin is standing across from me. I freeze.

He stares at me, his expression impossible to read. I swallow. I want to step back, but I force myself to stand my ground. I'm not going to let him bully me. Right now this is my kitchen. He can't boss me around here.

"What are you doing, Austin?" I ask. I'm glad my voice doesn't shake.

"Making dessert, Jelly Roll?" Austin asks. He looks at the counter. He eyes the pile of apples I still need to skin and slice.

"Pie rolls," I tell him. He steps up to the counter. My heart pounds hard in my chest when he grabs the knife lying next to the fruit. He grips the handle. I make sure I have a clear way to the exit.

"I used to make apple pies with my dad," Austin says. His words are quiet as he lifts the knife. He grabs an apple. He cuts into it and starts peeling off the skin.

My head is dizzy with relief and confusion. I watch him for a moment, stunned. He knows what he's doing. He expertly peels off the skin and slices the apple. I take a deep breath before I continue making the pastry.

"I make apple pies with my dad too," I say after a minute.

Austin grunts. "I said *used to*. My dad doesn't do anything with me anymore. Not since..."

I look at him. His head is lowered over the counter.

"You don't like his girlfriend?" I ask. I don't know why I'm even talking to him. I should be telling him to leave me alone. But he's doing a good job cutting up the apple. Besides, I've never seen Austin like this before. He doesn't look angry or scary. He looks sad.

"She doesn't like me," Austin says. He finishes the first apple and starts on another. "That's why she sent me here. She wanted to get rid of me for a while. So she could have my dad all to herself."

"Oh." I don't know what to say. I can't imagine how it would feel to be totally ignored by your parents, to not feel wanted. "Does your dad know about our stall idea for tomorrow?"

"No," Austin says. "He wouldn't care. He'll come by to pick me up. I bet he won't even ask what we did."

"You could tell him," I say. "When he comes to pick you up, you can bring him to the food truck. We're going to do a good job tomorrow. Think about it. What if our stall raised the most money out of everyone here? Wouldn't your dad be proud of that?"

Austin pauses mid-slice. His head tilts to one side as he thinks about what I've said.

"Maybe," he mutters at last. He says it like he might actually agree with me.

Austin slices the rest of the second apple and grabs a third. I don't say anything else as I finish making the pastry. We work side by side in silence. When all of the apples are sliced, Austin drops the knife on the counter and leaves without a word.

Chapter Fourteen

I go to the market early the next morning. The Young Leaders won't open their stalls for another three hours. But I want to make sure there is plenty of time to set up. I unlock the food truck and get the generator going. It will take a while for the fridge to get cold enough. We'll keep all the food we prepared inside the main building until the truck's ready.

The rest of my team will be coming over a little closer to opening time. For now I'm the only Granite County Young Leader who has arrived. There are already a few vendors in the market though. I pass meat counters and smell freshly baked bread in the building's main area. I also walk by a stall full of jam and jelly jars. But it is quiet in the hallway leading to the kitchen.

At least, it is nearly quiet. The farther I walk down the hallway, the more aware I am of thrashing and thudding noises in the distance. When I reach the kitchen door, I know the noises are coming from inside. My skin breaks out in a cold sweat as I turn the knob and pull the door open.

The kitchen is trashed. The small table and its two chairs have been knocked over. Knives, forks and spoons are strewn across the floor. The fridge is open. All of our food has been taken out. Blueberry filling is smeared across the counter. Cold cuts and lettuce have been dumped onto the table. One of the walls is smeared with orange goo. Someone obviously threw all the peach pie rolls at it.

And in the middle of the destruction is Austin. He hasn't noticed me yet.

He kicks at the open fridge door. The impact of his foot makes the whole appliance shake.

"Too busy to pick me up?" he mutters as the door hits the wall and swings back so he can kick it again. "Well, maybe you'll come when they tell you I've been kicked out!" He picks up a tray full of pie rolls. They're filled with the apples he helped me prepare last night. The memory of him slicing fruit as he talked about his dad makes my stomach hurt.

Austin lifts his arm and turns like he's preparing to throw the tray across the room. He stops when he sees me standing in the doorway. His hair is disheveled, and his eyes are red. He looks like he's been crying.

"What are you doing?" I ask in a wobbly voice. So much for rule number one. Looks like I'm going to cry too.

Austin seems embarrassed to have been caught. For a second he seems sorry as well. He blinks a few times before he rubs his eyes on his shirt sleeve. Then he sneers at me.

"I told you going against me was a bad idea, Jelly Roll," he says. He hurls the tray against the wall to my left. Apple filling explodes across the white cinder block. Gooey apple slices ooze down the wall. I cringe at the thought of all that wasted food. I jump when Austin pushes past me.

When he's out of sight, I slump down against the nearest wall and stare at the kitchen. Everything is ruined. There is no way we can do the food truck now.

After all of our hard work, Austin has still managed to win.

"That is what I get for trying to stand up to him," I whisper, even though I'm the only one in the room. "Katrina was right. People like him always get their way."

I want to go home. I want to call my dad. I want him to drive me and The Hungry Pup out of the parking lot and forget all about this stupid retreat.

I think again of Austin slicing apples. He wanted to make his dad proud. I want to make mine proud too. Dad wouldn't want me to quit. And I don't want Austin to win.

I sit up and wipe my eyes. Then I pull out my phone and check the time. Two and a half hours left until we have to open our stalls. If I work fast, I might be able to pull something else together. If I don't at least try, Austin will always know he beat me down when it mattered most.

"He's not going to get his way," I say as I pull myself up. "Not this time." I turn toward the door, ready to storm out of the room.

I nearly run into Ollie. He takes one step into the kitchen and then stops, a horrified expression on his face.

"What happened?" he asks.

I grab his arm and twist him around so he is looking at me. I don't want his focus to be on the disaster inside the kitchen. "An animal got in," I lie.

Ollie's eyebrows raise in surprise. "An *animal* did all this?"

"No," I admit. I stare into Ollie's eyes, and it doesn't take long for him to understand who really tore the kitchen apart.

"I can't believe that little—"

"Raccoon got in. I know," I say, cutting him off.

He looks at me, confused. "Why would you lie and say it was a raccoon? We need to tell the counselors what Austin did."

"No," I say again. I look around at the messy kitchen before I move to close the door. I don't want to risk anyone overhearing us. "If they know who the culprit really is, they might pull the plug on our project. And that might cause enough commotion to ruin the whole farmers' market." I don't want the counselors involved. Austin is expecting to get in trouble. And I know it would only make things between him and his dad worse. Despite all he's done, a part of me still feels sorry for him.

"So?" Ollie is furious. If Austin were here right now, Ollie would probably start throwing punches. "All of our stuff has been destroyed. We can't serve anything anyway."

"Austin wants us to fail," I tell him. "He wants us to give up. So that is exactly what we are not going to do."

"But how are we going to run the food truck without any food?" Ollie asks.

I take a deep breath, trying not to get overwhelmed by the amount of work we have in front of us. "We don't have the money to buy all the ingredients again. But if we focus on one recipe..."

I think about the other vendors in the market. When I remember the stall full of local jams and jellies, my heart starts to race. I have the perfect idea.

Ollie watches as I hurry to grab my backpack.

"What are we going to do?" he asks.

I head toward the hallway, grinning as I open the kitchen door. "Leave that to me. You stay here. I'm going to need your help. I'll be back soon."

Chapter Fifteen

Katrina said there was a grocery store down the road. I leave the market building and jog all the way to it. The air is cold, but the morning is bright. It gives me hope. My head is as clear as the sky. I know exactly what I need to do.

I use the remaining money from our budget to buy the supplies I need. Two kinds of sugar. Eggs and salt. Flour and baking powder. Vanilla, cocoa and butter. The store has everything I need. I grab a couple rolls of parchment paper on my way to the cash register.

Once I've stocked up, I head back to the farmers' market. I stop by the food truck to gather cooking utensils. Then I return to the main building. I head for the stall I'd noticed earlier. I pick a few jars of the strawberry preserves lined up on the table. I give the woman the last of my money and run back to the kitchen.

Ollie is washing up the trays the pie rolls were on. He fires questions at me, curious about what I have in mind.

"What you're doing right now is great," I tell him. "I'll need a few of those pans soon." I set out mixing bowls and lay parchment paper on a baking tray. "You'll see what I'm planning soon enough."

I mix sugar and butter. I crack in eggs and add vanilla. I whisk in flour, baking powder and salt. I scoop in cocoa to give the batter some chocolate flavor. While the oven is preheating, I pour the batter into the pans Ollie has cleaned. Then I start on the icing.

By the time the other kids arrive, the first batch of cake is cooling on a rack. I spread whipped icing over its length. Then I open the first jar of jelly.

"What is she doing?" Audrey asks as she steps into the kitchen. "Where is all our stuff?" Katrina and Sarah are with her. Meera is off setting up her snack station.

"We have had a change of plans," Ollie tells them. "But everything is under control." He explains what happened this morning as I finish up. I'm almost ready to unveil my new recipe.

I smooth the strawberry preserve over the icing. Then I roll up the cake. I sprinkle icing sugar and cocoa powder on top. Then I carefully slice into the roll. Each piece is a lovely spiral of chocolate cake, vanilla icing and strawberries. It has turned out perfectly.

I place one slice on a plate before turning and presenting it to my friends.

"I give you Roll Over's single menu item," I say. "A classic strawberry jelly roll, made with local strawberry preserves."

"Please tell me you need someone to do a taste test," Sarah says with big eyes. "Because I totally volunteer."

I laugh. "I thought you could all share. We need to make some money today!"

Sarah looks disappointed. "Yeah, I guess that makes sense," she says.

I smile. "If you like it, you can buy yourself another slice from the truck," I tell her.

"That's true," she says, perking up again.

I grab enough forks so everyone can try the dessert. As each person takes their first bite, I hold my breath. When I see their smiles, a shiver of excitement runs up my spine.

"This is delicious," Ollie says, scooping a second huge forkful into his mouth.

"I will definitely be ordering another one of these," Sarah says, mouth full of cake. A bit of jelly dribbles down her chin. She wipes it away with her finger and licks it off.

"It's only one item, but it totally goes with the name of the truck," I say. "If we take down the menu sign, no one will ever know we intended to serve other things. Roll Over will be the exclusive home of this exclusive jelly roll."

"Do we have enough supplies?" Ollie asks.

"We've got a ton of ingredients to bake more batches of cake," I say. "I'll stay in here and keep baking as we go."

"I can draw a new sign," Audrey says. "One just for the jelly roll."

"And then Audrey and I can be in the truck handing out slices," says Ollie. "I think this is going to work!" He sounds surprised. He looks it too.

"I know it will," I tell him. "But we need to get going."

Katrina nods. "I'll help you finish cleaning up before I go join my team," she says.

"I'll help too," Sarah adds. She has taken the rest of the slice for herself and has nearly finished it. "My team is selling produce bags made from old T-shirts that people can use for shopping at the market. They won't care if I'm a little late."

"Thank you," I say to them both.

Everyone starts moving at the same time. Ollie goes to prepare the cash drawer, and Audrey leaves to make her last sign. Katrina fills the sink so she can wash the rest of the utensils that Austin tossed on the floor. Sarah and I bring the first batch of rolls out to the food truck.

As we walk across the parking lot, I see Austin leaning against the building's brick wall. He doesn't look smug. When our eyes meet, he doesn't even bother to sneer. He clutches his phone, like he is waiting for a call he knows isn't really going to come. He looks lonely.

I'm not sure whether I feel sorry for him or glad to see him beaten. I think it is probably a bit of both.

Chapter Sixteen

I get the next batch of cake in the oven half an hour before our food truck opens. And then I don't stop baking for the rest of the day.

The cold doesn't stop people from lining up at our truck. Serving cake doesn't hurt either. The morning starts with a couple of people happy to donate their money to the food bank in exchange for something sweet. But then word catches on, and more and more people start to line up. We go through the first batch. And the second. And the third.

Eventually we run out of supplies and are forced to officially shut down the food truck. I'm exhausted from the nonstop baking. But I'm so happy, I start to cry for the second time today.

"That was amazing," Audrey says as she draws a SOLD OUT sign. She has jelly smudges on her forehead and a bit of dried icing on the tip of her nose. "I can't believe how busy we were."

Ollie nods. "At least five people asked if we will be serving jelly rolls at the market next week," he says.

"I didn't even get to buy mine," Sarah says, pouting. She has been back and forth between her stall and the food truck all day.

I smile as I open the cupboard over my head. I reach into the back and pull out the mini cake roll I stashed there a few hours ago when I didn't have enough batter to make a full-sized one.

"I hoped it would be a success," I say, taking a small container of icing and preserves from the fridge. "And I planned accordingly so we could celebrate. I have enough to make us all a slice. Katrina and Meera too."

Sarah bounces on her toes. She hurries to find me a spreader. Together we make the last jelly roll. Ollie and Audrey eat their slices in the truck while Sarah goes off in search of Katrina and Meera. I grab mine and take it outside. After hours in the kitchen, I'm desperate for some fresh air.

I walk past the other outdoor vendors still selling their wares. There is a park nearby, and I head toward the nearest empty picnic table. I don't even stop when I see Austin at the next table over.

He is hunched over his phone. When I'm close I can hear him mumbling. He pulls his arm back like he is going to hurl the phone the same way he hurled the pie rolls earlier. When he looks up and sees me, he stops. For a second he looks embarrassed again. Then he just looks tired.

"You didn't tell the counselors what I did," he says.

I shrug my shoulders. "I didn't want to ruin the market."

Austin sighs. He stares down at his phone again. "Yeah well, now I have to take a three-hour bus ride home," he says. "And I can't even get the schedule to load on this stupid phone."

"Sorry your dad didn't come," I say.

Austin rolls his eyes. "Whatever."

Why am I even bothering to be nice? I can't stand Austin. And I certainly don't forgive him for all the horrible stuff he has done. But I don't want to be like him. I guess that is why.

"Here," I say. I hold out my slice of cake. He looks at it like it's poisoned. I'm tempted to take it back and eat it myself. But I want him to try it. I want him to know it's good.

I place the cake on the table beside him. Then I start to turn away.

"I guess I shouldn't be surprised you know your way around a kitchen," Austin says behind me. I look back to see him picking up the plate. He takes a bite, and then he nods. "This is pretty good."

"I figured you'd like it." I keep talking before I have time to chicken out of saying the rest. "You spend so much of your time obsessing over jelly rolls, I figured they must be your favorite."

Austin raises his eyebrows, stunned at my words. I guess I'm breaking all the rules today. Austin's seen me cry. And now he's heard my comeback too.

He gets off the park bench. I hold my breath as he walks toward me. As brave as I want to be, it is hard not to feel nervous when he gets close. He stops in front of me. His eyes stare into mine, but they are not so cold under the sunny sky. For a second Austin sneers at me. But then his face falls, and he only looks sorry.

"Do you need any help cleaning up?" he asks in a quiet voice.

The question surprises me. We've already cleaned up after Austin. I almost tell him we don't want his help. But the food truck is a mess. Austin didn't take part in making anything. It seems fitting he should at least help with the dishes.

"Yes, we do," I say with a nod. I place one hand on my hip and point in the direction of the truck. "You can finish your dessert and then wash all the baking pans. You'll have to scrub hard. I don't want any cake crumbs left over."

I'm not used to sounding bossy. It's kind of fun.

Austin looks at the food truck. Then he shrugs his shoulders and steps around me. Before he passes, I catch the hint of a smile on his lips. "Whatever you say, J.R." He walks off, eating another bite of cake as he goes.

I let out a long breath as I watch him walk away. *Never* has Austin called me anything other than Jelly Roll when no one else was around. School is back in tomorrow, and I'm going to have my work cut out for me. Austin and his friends will still be mean. But their teasing won't break me. I think Austin knows that now.

Because, as it turns out, being a Jelly Roll is actually pretty sweet.

Mere Joyce is the author of several novels for young people, including *Shadow* from the Orca Currents line. She lives in Kitchener, Ontario, with her family.

For more information on all the books

in the Orca Currents line, please visit

orcabook.com.